Andy's Adventure

Written by Shelly Peters
Illustrated by Jeff McKellar and Walt Wilcox

This is Andy.

This is Andy the athlete.

This is Andy the acrobat.

This is Andy the astronaut.

This is Andy the actor.

This is Andy the alligator.

Andy is in the attic.